Squeaky Cleaners

in a stew!

Vivian French

illustrated by

Anna Currey

Hodder
Children's
Books

a division of Hodder Headline plc

To Cally, with love
Vivian French

To Elinor
Anna Currey

Text copyright © Vivian French 1996
Illustration copyright © Anna Currey 1996

This edition published as a My First Read Alone in 1998
by Hodder Children's Books

First published in Great Britain in 1996
by Hodder Children's Books

10 9 8 7 6 5 4

ISBN 0 340 72666 0

Printed and bound in Great Britain by
The Devonshire Press Ltd, Torquay, Devon TQ2 7NX

Hodder Children's Books
a division of Hodder Headline plc
338 Euston Road
London NW1 3BH

One

'Eeek,' said Nina. She was sitting at the
table and counting the money from the
money-box. 'There's nothing here
except pennies. No cheese pie tonight.'

Gina looked up from her knitting.
'What was that, dear?'

'We need more money,' said Nina.

'Oh my goodness me!' Gina dropped
her ball of wool. 'Oh, whatever shall
we do?'

4

Fred opened one eye, and then
closed it again.

Nina picked up the wool and
handed it back to Gina. 'Keep your
whiskers on,' she said. 'I'm sure
something will turn up.'

Gina peered anxiously at the
telephone. 'But we haven't had a call for
ages and ages! Maybe we won't be able
to buy any cheese ever again!'
BRRRINGGGGGGGGGGG!

Gina squeaked loudly and dropped
her ball of wool for the second time.

'Hurrah!' said Nina, and she picked up the telephone. 'Squeaky Cleaners. Nina speaking – can I help you?'

There was a muffled noise from the other end of the line.

'What's that?' Nina asked. 'Cleaning?
Oh yes, we clean houses from top to
bottom and bottom to top. Today? Well,
yes – we might be able to fit you in.
Twenty-seven Daisy Road? Thank you.
See you soon!'

Nina put down the telephone. 'There
you are. I said something would turn up.'

8

Gina wound up her knitting. 'So you did, dear. What a relief! So who was it?'

Nina pulled at her ear. 'Well,' she said, 'it's not one of our usual customers . . .'

'Fancy!' said Gina. 'Someone new. How lovely!'

'Yes,' said Nina. She took a deep breath. 'It's Miss Kitty Plush!'

Gina let out such a loud squeal that Fred sat bolt upright.

'What's going on?' he asked.

Gina sat down and fanned herself
with her paws. 'Oh, Fred! Nina has said
we'll go and clean the house of a *cat*!'

Nina nodded. 'There'll be no supper tonight if we don't!'

Fred twirled his tail. 'I'd like to see the cat that can catch *me*!' he said.

'Oh! Oh! Oh!' moaned Gina.

Two

In Twenty-seven Daisy Road Miss Kitty Plush was skipping round her kitchen.

'Purrr! Purrr! Purrr! What a clever little pussy cat I am! Tonight I shall cook a mouse stew. Mother will think I am such a good kitten!' She purred happily.

'I shall tell the dear little Squeaky Cleaners to clean up and down and all around. Then, when everything is spicky-span and shining, I shall bounce and pounce on them and pop them in my nice mouse stew!'

Three

Nina was loading up the van with buckets and dusters and brooms and dustpans.

Fred was polishing his motorbike.

Gina was leaning
on a mop and
feeling pale. Her
whiskers were
drooping, and
her tail was
limp.

'Cheer up, Gina!' Nina said. 'Think
of the wonderful cheese pie we can
make when we get home with a pocket
full of wages.'

'If we haven't been made into mouse pie,' Fred said cheerfully.

Gina began to tremble.

'*Be quiet*, Fred!' Nina hissed.

'Only joking,' said Fred. He took Gina's mop and slung it in the back of the van. 'In you hop, Gina! I'll see you there!' He jumped on to his motorbike and roared away.

Nina started the engine. 'Stop worrying, Gina,' she said. 'We'll be home again in no time at all!'

'If we haven't been eaten,' Gina said, and blew her nose loudly.

Four

Miss Kitty Plush did not hear Fred roar up on his motorbike. She was peering closely at a cookery book and muttering to herself.

'Oh, my patty paws!' she said.
'Mouse stew is very difficult.'
PINGGGGGGGGGGGGG!

Miss Kitty jumped and dropped her
cookery book.

'Meeow!' she said. 'I do hope these
mice are fat little mice!'

She hurried to open the front door.
Miss Kitty looked at the Squeaky
Cleaners.

'Such *fat* – I mean, such *kind* little
mice,' she purred. '*Do* come in.'

The Squeaky Cleaners stepped inside.

Miss Kitty locked the door behind them.

'Please excuse me,' she said. 'I must
get on with cooking my – my – oh dear.
I mean – I must cook a little fishy pie.
Ahem.'

Nina glanced round. Miss Kitty Plush was not a tidy cat. There were fish-bones and fluff and dust everywhere.

'I think we'll begin at the top of the house,' she said.

'Lovely,' said Miss Kitty, and
she smiled. Gina thought her teeth
looked extremely white and sharp.

'We'll start at once, then,' said Nina.
She gave Gina a push, and Gina
squeaked and scampered up the stairs.
At the top of the stairs Gina sank
down. She looked very pale, and
her whiskers trembled. Nina
fanned her with a large duster.

'Come on, Gina,' she said. 'The sooner we begin, the sooner we can go home!'

Gina staggered to her feet and took the broom with quivering paws.

'Did you see her teeth?' she quavered. 'Like needles!'

Fred waved a duster. 'All the better to eat us with!'

'Fred!' said Nina.

'Sorry,' said Fred, and he picked up the tin of polish.

Five

An hour later Nina and Gina were still
busy. They had swept and scrubbed and
polished the top of the house, and now
they were busy in the middle.

Gina was feeling better. The sight of shining floors and gleaming windows always cheered her up. She even hummed a little as she swept.

Fred was tired of dusting. He was also tired of Gina telling him to work harder. He tiptoed down the stairs, sniffing.

'That's never fishy pie that's cooking
in the kitchen,' he said to himself.
'There's not so much as a whiff of fish.'

He went a little further. 'So why did
Miss Kitty Plush tell a lie?' He sniffed

again. 'Onions? Yes. Carrots? Yes. Gravy? Yes.' He nodded. 'Mouse stew. That's what it is. Mouse stew . . . but without the mice. Hmm.' And Fred sat down on the bottom step to plot and plan.

There was a loud CRASH from the kitchen. It was followed by a loud MERROW and the smell of burning onions.

Fred stood up, and strolled into the kitchen.

Miss Kitty was sucking her paw. She glared at a smoking saucepan.

The cookery book lay in a pool
of gravy.

'Why, Miss Kitty!' said Fred.
'Is something wrong?'

Miss Kitty burst into tears.

'MEEEOW!' she howled. 'I wanted to make a lovely dinner for my mummy, but it won't go right!'

Fred shook his head. 'Mouse stew is very difficult,' he said.

Miss Kitty stopped crying and stared at Fred. 'How did you know I was making mouse stew?'

Fred sighed. 'I smelt it. Onions, carrots and gravy. The trouble is, the cookery book never tells you how to do it the easy way.'

Miss Kitty wiped her eyes on her tail.
'Is there an easy way?'

'Oh yes,' said Fred. 'Very easy. Nice
mouse stew. Shall we show you?'

Miss Kitty nodded.

'One moment,' said Fred, 'and I'll fetch Nina and Gina.' And he scampered away up the stairs.

Six

It took Fred and Nina five whole
minutes to persuade Gina to come
downstairs. It was only when they
promised that she could hold on to the
largest mop that they got her to creep
into the kitchen.

'You've been a very long time,' Miss Kitty said crossly. 'Something else has burnt now.'

It was true. The carrots were black.

'Never mind,' said Nina. 'We'll have you sorted out in no time.'

The three mice scurried about. Miss Kitty Plush watched in wonder as a neat pile of vegetables grew and grew.

'Good!' said Fred. 'What next, Nina?'

Nina pretended to think hard. 'Gently fry the onions. Oh, and we should get the nice mice ready. You have got the right kind, haven't you, Miss Kitty?'

Miss Kitty Plush opened her eyes very wide.

'Is there a wrong kind of mouse?' she asked.

'Oh *yes!*' said Fred and Nina together. Gina nodded.

'We're the wrong kind,' Fred said.
'We'd taste of soap and polish.
Disgusting! What you need is fat, tender
little mice fed on cheese, and bacon,
and breadcrumbs. Yum yum!'

'Ah,' said Miss Kitty. 'Are you sure?'

'Oh yes!' said Nina. '*Quite* sure.'

'Oh,' said Miss Kitty. 'But I haven't got any nice mice!'

She began to wail. 'Meeow, meeow.
Now I won't have any lovely mouse
stew for my mummy!'

Fred looked at Nina. Nina looked at Fred. Gina held her breath.

'I suppose we could help,' Fred said slowly. 'I mean, we do have the van outside.'

'It wouldn't take us long,' said Nina.
'Not long,' gasped Gina.

Fred threw down his wooden spoon.

'All right! Just for you, Miss Kitty!
We'll pop out and fetch you a couple of
nice little mice. Nice little mice for your
nice mouse stew! Open the door, and
we'll be back in two shakes of a
whisker!'

Miss Kitty Plush hurried to unlock
the door. She waved at the Squeaky
Cleaners as they tumbled down the steps.

She watched Fred screech off on his
motorbike, and Nina and Gina roar off
in the van.

'What *dear* little mice,' she thought
to herself. 'What nice little mice!'
Miss Kitty Plush stood very still.

'Oh! MEEOW MEEOW MEEOW.
COME BACK, COME BACK. Oh, I've
been tricked! I've been tricked!'

And Miss Kitty Plush went back to
her kitchen to cry.

Seven

Fred arrived home first. Nina and Gina
were close behind.

'Phew!' said Fred. 'What a busy day!'
Gina sank down in her chair.

Nina began tidying away the brushes and brooms.

'Well done, Fred,' she said. 'What will Miss Kitty Plush say when she finds out we're not coming back?'

Fred grinned. 'What will she say when she finds out the rest of her onions and carrots are missing too?' And he patted his bulging pockets.

'Oh, Fred!' said Gina.

'Vegetable stew for us tonight!' said Fred.

'Stew for the nicest mice!' said Nina, and they all laughed.